BAU
D0131438
WITHDRAWN
CARSON CITY LIBRARY

The Longest Night

The Longest Night

by Marion Dane Bauer
illustrated by Ted Lewin

Holiday House / New York

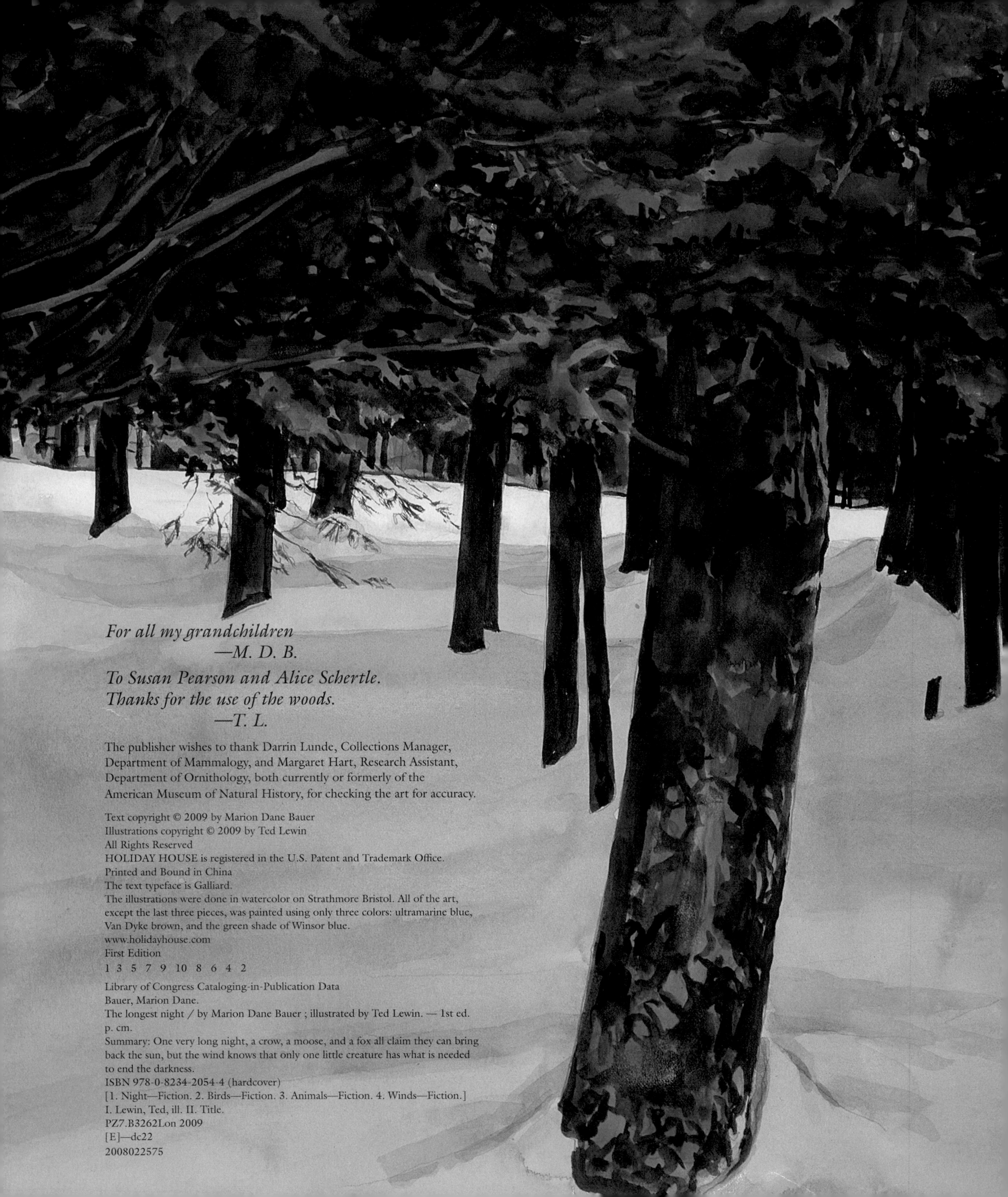

For all my grandchildren
—M. D. B.

To Susan Pearson and Alice Schertle.
Thanks for the use of the woods.
—T. L.

The publisher wishes to thank Darrin Lunde, Collections Manager, Department of Mammalogy, and Margaret Hart, Research Assistant, Department of Ornithology, both currently or formerly of the American Museum of Natural History, for checking the art for accuracy.

Text copyright © 2009 by Marion Dane Bauer
Illustrations copyright © 2009 by Ted Lewin
All Rights Reserved
HOLIDAY HOUSE is registered in the U.S. Patent and Trademark Office.
Printed and Bound in China
The text typeface is Galliard.
The illustrations were done in watercolor on Strathmore Bristol. All of the art, except the last three pieces, was painted using only three colors: ultramarine blue, Van Dyke brown, and the green shade of Winsor blue.
www.holidayhouse.com
First Edition
1 3 5 7 9 10 8 6 4 2

Library of Congress Cataloging-in-Publication Data
Bauer, Marion Dane.
The longest night / by Marion Dane Bauer ; illustrated by Ted Lewin. — 1st ed.
p. cm.
Summary: One very long night, a crow, a moose, and a fox all claim they can bring back the sun, but the wind knows that only one little creature has what is needed to end the darkness.
ISBN 978-0-8234-2054-4 (hardcover)
[1. Night—Fiction. 2. Birds—Fiction. 3. Animals—Fiction. 4. Winds—Fiction.]
I. Lewin, Ted, ill. II. Title.
PZ7.B3262Lon 2009
[E]—dc22
2008022575

The snow lies deep.
The night is long and long.
The stars are ice, the moon is frost,
and all the world is still.

Bears sleep, as do the velvet mice.
A moon shadow lies by every tree,
thin as a hungry wolf.
"Sha-a-a," whines the wind, the bitter wind.
"Cold and dark now rule.
Cold and dark now rule!"

"Gone!" caws the crow, the night-dark crow.
"So long the sun's been gone.
I saw it slink,
I saw it sneak,
I saw it creep behind a cloud
and go to sleep.
But I'm the one.

I know how to bring back the sun.
I'll fly with my strong wings
to reach the clouds.
I'll poke with my sharp beak
and wake the sun."
"Not you," sighs the wind. "Not you."

“Gone!” cries the moose, the mighty moose.
“I know the sun is gone!
I saw it slip,
I saw it slide,
I saw it plunge
from the bowl of the sky
and disappear behind a hill.

But I'm the one.
I know how to bring back the sun.
I have legs long enough
to reach that hill,
to climb that hill.
I have antlers strong enough
to scoop up the sun
and bring it home."
"Not you," sighs the wind. "Not you."

"Gone!" barks the fox, the clever fox.
"The sun is too long gone.
Someone must search,
someone must seek,
someone must find the hole
the sun crawled into.

I'm the one.
I know how to bring back the sun.
I have a nose keen enough
to sniff out the sun's hiding place,
paws quick enough
to dig it up,
teeth sharp enough
to grab the sun and toss it back into the sky."
"Not you," sighs the wind. "Not you.
Sha-shee. Sha-shoo."

“The night is long and long,” says a chickadee.
“The sun is gone and gone.
If not crow or moose or fox, then who?
Who can bring back the sun?”
“You,” says the wind. “Only you.”

“Me?” cries the chickadee.
“Her?” cry crow and moose and fox.
“Sha-shoo,” answers the wind.
Chickadee hears,
“Only you.”

The little bird knows
she can't fly all the way to the sun.
Her beak isn't strong enough to poke it awake.
She can't climb or scoop.
She can't sniff or dig or toss the sun into the sky.
So she does instead what chickadees do best.
She sings a song.
"Dee-dee-dee," she sings.
"And dee and dee and dee," she sings.
"And dee and dee, again."

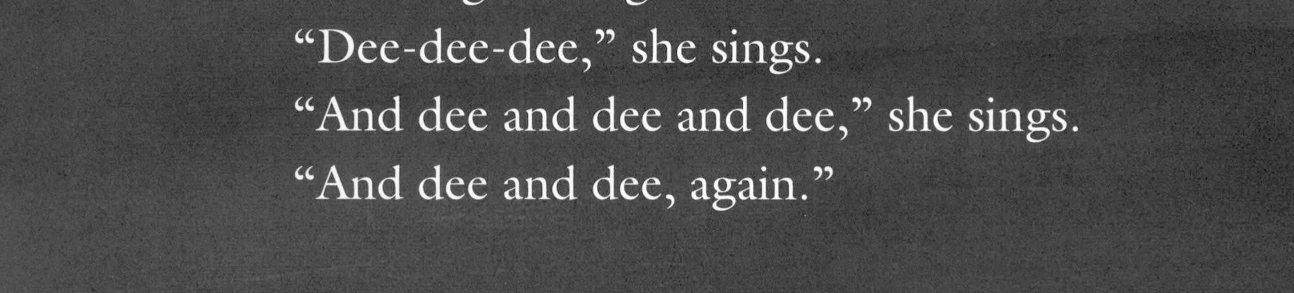

"What kind of noise is that?" cries crow.
"Just dee and dee and dee."
"The sun won't listen to such nonsense,"
bellows moose.
"What can it possibly mean?" barks fox.
"Just dee," says the chickadee.
"Only that.
Dee-dee-dee."
"Sha-shee," says the wind.

A star melts away,
then another.
The frosty moon pauses,
snagged in the branches of a tree.
The world holds its breath . . . waiting.

"Dee-dee-dee," says the chickadee.
And again, "Dee and dee."

Slowly, slowly, the sun opens his eyes.
He stretches.
He tilts his head, listening.
"Who sings in the cold and dark?" he asks.
"Who indeed?" whispers the wind.
"Sha-shee . . . sha-shoo!"
"Dee-dee-dee," says the chickadee.
And the sun smiles.

Fingers of light
peel back the blanket of darkness.
Fingers of light
grasp the edge of the world,
and slowly, slowly,
the sun lifts himself
into the sky.

"Thank you, sun!"
sings the chickadee.
"Thank you, sun!"
echoes the world.

And with the song
of one small bird
and the sun's answering smile
the journey toward spring
begins.